LAST EPISODE
by
K. E. Adamus

Also by K. E. Adamus

Can a gym be a place for epoch-making discoveries, on par with a "Eureka!" moment? It's quite possible that someone, while plodding away on a treadmill, suddenly came up with a profitable business idea. Someone else might have thought up a topic for a newspaper article.

Mark's discovery was of a smaller caliber, though it turned his stable life upside down.

For the first time in ages, he had managed to convince his wife to work out with him. He thought she'd be lifting weights by his side. Admiring his muscles. Training with him on every machine in turn.

But Ilona had been stubbornly pedaling away on the stationary bike for half an hour.

Between his own sets and while switching machines, Mark kept walking over to her and trying to chat, but she brushed him off with one-word answers.

While working his thigh muscles, he suddenly felt a lump in his throat. He had just noticed two muscular men entering the workout area. Were they warming up near Ilona?

Had she spotted some guy in the other room and that's why she didn't want to work out with him?

He didn't get injured only thanks to the habit he had developed over time of handling gym machines with care. The weights crashed down with force, and he rushed into the other room. He looked around, furious.

This room housed the stationary bikes and treadmills.

Half of the treadmills were empty. The rest were occupied by women. Instinctively, he glanced at their buttocks, tightly wrapped in snug shorts. He had to admit—they looked more appealing than his wife's.

It hadn't always been that way.

He looked at his wife. Not tired at all, she was gently moving her legs, pedaling on the lowest resistance. Her eyes were fixed on the small TV screen mounted on the bike.

Next to her, some grey-haired old man was pushing his personal world record.

At first, he thought there was no threat at all. But after a moment, he began asking himself—does Ilona prefer older men? Then, in the angled mirror, he caught sight of a muscular silhouette. He spun around in fury, looking for a rival. It took him a full second to realize he had seen his own reflection.

Ilona had reluctantly agreed to go to the gym with him. Her old tracksuit had gotten too tight, and the accumulated rolls of fat showed through. She felt unattractive—especially when comparing herself to the other women in the room.

She tried to comfort herself with the thought that those women were probably athletic, had firm bodies, but were dumb. However, that stereotype had to collapse and die a natural death the moment she overheard a conversation between two women about molecules. They were two attractive blondes, speaking with articulate, refined language.

Ilona suddenly felt like an unattractive ignoramus. She knew very little about molecules. And yet she had always considered herself intelligent, well-informed, skillful, with a sharp sense of humor.

After just five minutes, she had already fixed her gaze on the tiny screen of the exercise bike, watching music videos with growing horror, comparing the slim, beautiful singers to herself.

Half an hour later, Mark burst into the room.

He had always been so tender and warm. Maybe this time, too, he would help her relieve the stress brought on by the sudden realization of her own ignorance and her slightly overweight body.

"Marky!" she began sweetly as he approached her bike. "Tell me, do you think my jokes are funny?"

"So you think this is funny!" Mark shouted, drawing the attention of nearly everyone in the room—especially the women, whose focus lingered. "Well, know this—I'm not laughing at all!"

"What?" Ilona asked, confused. "I haven't even told a joke yet."

"You *are* the joke," Mark muttered, and instantly regretted his words. He had always tried to be kind to Ilona, even in tense or patience-testing moments.

Ilona pouted, deeply offended. Two tears slipped down from beneath her unpainted lashes.

She also began pedaling more vigorously.

The other women were delighted. Maybe this amazing guy would argue with "the Fat One" even more, finally dump her, and become available. What did he need a hag like that for?

Meanwhile, inside the "hag's" head, a void had formed. All she felt was deep sadness—and the sense that something in their relationship had ended.

"Why aren't you working out on the machines?" Mark decided to go on the offensive. Supposedly, attack is better than defense.

"Because I'm working out on the bike," Ilona grumbled.

"And what does the bike have that the machines don't?"

"Television!" Ilona shouted. "I'd rather watch TV than listen to you wheezing while you bench press."

"You watch TV all the time! You don't do anything else!"

And at that moment, Mark made his discovery. His wife was addicted to television. Even in the morning, when she was making him breakfast, she seemed absent—completely absorbed by whatever show was on TV.

Occasionally, she'd say things like: *"Did you hear what she just said?"* or *"Did you see that?"*

Mark was usually busy reviewing his calendar, so he always gave the same reply: *"Yes, darling."* There was never any follow-up question, so he felt safe planning his day.

When he came home, dinner would be ready—or nearly so. His wife would apologize for the delay, explaining that she got caught up in front of the TV because something interesting was on.

During dinner, the television was always on. Ilona would ask how his day at work had gone, but he could simply reply, "Good," and the subject wouldn't be pushed any further. That suited him just fine, as he usually brought work home. His ambition was to edge out his boss and take over his position. After that, he figured he could ease up and start enjoying life. But while working toward that "later," he lost sight of his wife.

What was she doing while he holed up in the room he'd converted into his office? He thought maybe she was reading books or furthering her education. The truth was worse. Ilona only watched television. She wasn't addicted to the Internet, didn't chat with random men or arrange dates while he was at work—as he sometimes suspected. All Ilona needed to be happy were soap operas, talk shows, game shows, and then more series and movies in the evening. She rarely watched the news.

Whenever there was an important match involving the national team, he had to fight his own match—a battle for control of the TV, the remote, and the main armchair. Usually, he'd try to arrange a girls' night out for Ilona with her old friends. She herself showed no interest in such outings. Going out with his own mates wasn't an option—Ilona would get jealous. So he'd book a table at a restaurant, call her somewhat reluctant friends from university or her old job, and present her with a done deal. "It'll be fun for you!" he'd explain. "And I could use a guy's night too."

But that little maneuver worked maybe once a year. Ilona was offended by the idea that he might want to have fun without her. After such an evening, she'd usually try to engage him in conversation, pretending interest in his life, but soon enough, the TV routine would take over her world again.

And so, Mark experienced a sudden epiphany.

Ilona was furiously pedaling on her exercise bike, sniffling and staring at the TV screen.

"Honey, I think you might have a little problem," Mark began, trying to start a conversation.

"You *are* my main problem," Ilona sniffled in reply.

She instantly felt a bit better. She'd managed to get back at him for his rude comment, and her pride hurt a little less.

"Sweetheart, you watch too much television," Mark tried again.

"On TV, they don't even show egoists like you as villains!"

"You didn't used to be so mouthy. That TV has rotted your brain. We used to treat each other with respect. And now we're arguing in public. People are listening."

"Your argument isn't particularly interesting," wheezed the old man working out next to Ilona. "You both lack debate skills, structure, and your arguments are weak. Honestly, I have no idea what you're even fighting about. But you're disturbing everyone. People come here to relax."

Ilona blushed and walked out of the gym. As she got off the bike, though, she glanced at the music video channel—it was playing a song she liked. Mark followed her toward the exit. On their way out, two muscular men passed them. Mark looked at Ilona to see if she was checking them out.

"The old man was right!" Ilona said, sensing his gaze. "I can't even argue properly... I can't do *anything* right!"

"You can cook... and you can watch TV."

Ilona gave him a crooked smile.

"That skill is very useful, especially on the job market."

"Do you want to go back to work?" Mark asked. "I can ask around a bit."

"I don't feel ready yet... Besides, I have to watch TV."

"Your jokes are corny, but they make me laugh," Mark smiled. "My salary is enough for both of us, especially since your sick leave pay is kind of meager. You'll go back to work when you're feeling better."

He thought he had defused the argument. He was wrong.

"You don't have to throw money in my face!" Ilona shouted. "I'll get a job as a TV series analyst and get paid to watch them."

"Probably for reading scripts and screenplays..." Mark interjected.

"Of course! Mr. 'I-Know-Everything' always knows best."

"Now I'm not even sure if you're arguing about money or about who's smarter," came the old man's comment as he slipped past them on his way to the sauna. "Back in my day, the art of arguing was on par with that of ancient times."

"Off you go to your antiques, old man," Mark snapped, clearly irritated. He underestimated his opponent. The old man's fist landed squarely in his right eye socket with surprising force.

"Because honor is something you only get once!" the old man panted to the stunned Ilona. "They can take everything from you, but honor always remains."

Ilona looked at Mark with a mix of satisfaction and regret. She didn't like seeing him in the role of a victim. On the other hand, he deserved that punch for the "antique" comment. Actually, he kind of deserved everything.

Mark, dazed, was holding his rapidly swelling eye.

"How am I supposed to show up at work like this!" he groaned.

"Workaholic! Even now, all you can think about is work."

"I work because I enjoy it. And I'll work even more now. Even on weekends. I won't even take any vacation!"

He was wrong about that last part. His eye had swollen to the size of a tennis ball and turned purple. In that condition, he clearly couldn't compete for a promotion. He called work early in the morning and took a week of overdue vacation, while also scheduling various appointments aimed at eliminating the "tennis ball" from his eye socket as quickly as possible.

The only upside to the situation was the chance to observe Ilona's daily habits. At least, that was the plan. But Ilona seemed to sense the shift. She watched her usual morning show, but once it ended, she'd turn off the TV and pretend to do some exercise. It was obvious that even basic squats were a struggle for her. She clumsily tried to do a seated forward bend. Clearly, she had no practice—if she really did morning exercises regularly, it would have shown.

After these little performances, she would go out to buy groceries for lunch. She was gone for a long time. One day, he followed her and saw her entering the train station café, where—naturally—the TV was on. And of course, she wasn't just watching. At least one pastry had been eaten. That much he was sure of. What he couldn't confirm was how many.

After returning from her "shopping," Ilona would triumphantly turn the TV back on. *"I like having something buzzing in the background while I cook,"* she explained.

Then came the rituals he already knew well, since it was usually the time he came home from work—alternating between snacking and watching TV. Before their incident at the gym, she would occasionally speak to him sweetly, using pet names like *"teddy bear," "darling,"* or *"Marky."* Now she has stopped. Clearly, she was still offended.

Mark preferred to remain diplomatically silent and not touch the sensitive subject of television. But he kept making notes. His wife sat in front of the TV from six to nine in the morning. Then she'd turn it back on at 3:30 p.m. and leave it on until late at night. That meant she watched TV for at least eleven hours a day in his presence. And what about when he wasn't home? He didn't have to wonder long—he was sure the television stayed on all day.

By the end of his recovery week, he finally decided to bring up the topic.

"Sweetheart, researchers did a study and found that the average person spends several years of their life watching television..."

"And I spend half of my life watching it, and the other half sleeping? Is that what you're trying to say?"

"Something like that." Mark ventured.

"The TV is my window to the world. I sit at home, we never go anywhere because you're always working. Besides, I want to write screenplays, and I *have* to watch lots of shows to see how the competition does it. You understand, right?"

"Maybe you could just sign up for a screenwriting course?"

"Tarantino learned everything by watching movies on VHS tapes."

"Sweetheart, how many scenes are there in a class A film versus a class B film?"

"Why should I know that?" Ilona shrugged. "You have to feel it in your blood, have an artistic soul."

"And what kind of soul should a surgeon have?"

"The kind I have right now—ready to give you a black eye in the other socket!"

Mark gave up on the conversation and went to bed. Tomorrow was his first day back at work after a rather unusual absence—for him—and he preferred to get some sleep so he'd be ready to face the comebacks and snarky remarks from his coworkers.

Ilona began to reflect on Mark's words. She wasn't stupid. Maybe she really *was* watching too much television? *"But everyone does it!"* she justified herself inwardly. *"Everyone does it, or at least wishes they could."* All of her friends who didn't work. Even the ones who did would turn on the TV the moment they got home—and would complain when the unemployed friends quizzed them about the latest soap opera drama, saying *"We work, we don't sit at home all day."*

Ilona switched the channel to a music station. She couldn't concentrate on the plot of the film she'd been watching. Besides, if Mark came back to argue, she could say she was just listening to music, not watching TV. She began mentally replaying her daily routine.

At 6 a.m., the morning TV shows would start. The programs were interesting and, according to Ilona, *"broadened her mental horizons and knowledge."* That's what she always told Mark when he asked why she got up so early.

She would get up at 5:50. Run to the bathroom, brush her teeth, splash water on her face, and then rush to turn on the TV. The television was in the dining-living room area, which was open to the kitchen. The big screen suited the large space—and, most importantly, it was visible from the kitchen.

She would slowly prepare breakfast for herself and Mark. He got up at 6:30, locked himself in the bathroom for half an hour, and emerged freshly shaved and showered at exactly 7:00 for breakfast. He would eat everything she prepared in just 10 minutes. Then, for the next 10 minutes, he'd drink coffee while scribbling something in his calendar. After that, he'd jump up from the table, get dressed, and be out the door within 10 minutes.

The commute to work only took him 15 minutes, but Mark— as he always made clear—valued punctuality. For him, that meant not just walking into the office at eight, but already *sitting* at his desk, with a steaming cup of coffee beside him, ready to start the day.

"We don't even talk to each other anymore!" Ilona realized, replaying their morning routines in her head.

She was busy with the television. He was busy planning his day. They were missing each other.

It hadn't always been like that.

Instead of rushing to the TV, she used to cuddle up to Mark, and their mornings would begin with playful intimacy. Sometimes, they wouldn't even have time to make or eat breakfast together. They'd rush off to work hungry—but happy.

And now? She felt like an old hen.

They hadn't had sex in two years. Even couples married twenty years still had sex now and then—and they'd only been married five.

Was it her fault? She rushed to the TV in the morning and sat in front of it until night, long after Mark had already gone to bed.

But he would wake up when she got up. He *could* have pulled her back into bed.

Instead, he rolled over and preferred to sleep.

So between 6 and 9 a.m., there was the morning TV show. Then the news. And then came the midday telenovela paradise. There was plenty to choose from. She could always switch to cable or satellite channels.

She'd giggle at the agricultural programming schedule. *Who even watches that? Who cares?*

Sometimes she'd watch the news, but other times she'd switch to a lighter show, afraid of hearing bad tidings.

Mark came home from work at 4:30 p.m.

By then, she would either be cooking lunch—or pretending she had made all the necessary preparations.

While Mark was home, she kept the TV tuned to educational programs. She was ashamed of her weakness for soap operas. She wanted Mark to think of her as an ambitious person. But as soon as he locked himself away in his study, she would switch to the telenovela channels. After all, she was going to be a screenwriter one day. She had to observe the competition.

Around seven in the evening, Mark would come into the kitchen and fix himself something to eat. They didn't have the habit of sharing that meal together. Ilona was usually silently offended that Mark never prepared anything for her. After all, *she* made lunch and breakfast. And he only thought about himself. But she never brought it up. She was afraid of that kind of confrontation. After all, *she* was the one pretending to have depression and staying home all day, while he worked hard. She was the only one who knew it was fake. She hadn't even admitted it to Mark.

The truth was—she just hated her job. It consumed her mind and left her unable to focus on self-fulfillment. She decided to take a six-month leave to write a screenplay. Six months turned into two years, and she hadn't written a single page.

She gained weight because, when she quit her job, she also decided to quit smoking—something that had always annoyed Mark. She replaced cigarettes with food. She didn't exercise. And so, she gained 20 kilograms. No wonder Mark wasn't interested in sex anymore.

She felt a wave of resentment toward him. *Maybe... maybe I should try?*

With some hesitation, she walked into the bedroom. Mark was asleep. She slipped under the covers and began massaging his feet. It used to be their subtle signal that Ilona was in the mood for intimacy. She had always been shy and never good at expressing her needs directly.

"Well, finally," Mark murmured. "I've been waiting for this for a long time..."

And then Ilona suddenly remembered that the rerun of the episode she'd missed because of a dentist appointment was starting in five minutes.

Mumbling that she was *"just going to set the recording,"* she rushed to the TV.

By the time she returned, Mark's feet were covered with socks, and he was completely unmoved by her advances. Clearly, he was offended that he had lost out to the TV.

The tennis ball in Mark's eye socket had only slightly shrunk after a week. Still upset with Ilona, he decided to tell everyone at work that she had hit him. He thought it would be funny and that everyone would take it as a cheeky excuse hiding a darker, *Fight Club*-style truth.

But they believed him.

"You should get a divorce," his boss said, patting him on the shoulder. "No point in wasting your life."

Mark didn't know how to get out of the situation, so he chose to stay silent.

Around eleven o'clock, he decided to check what Ilona was doing. Was she at home watching TV? Or maybe she'd gone to the pastry shop? Or—was she *meeting someone* at that pastry shop?

He hadn't waited long that day. What if she had gone there for a secret date?

He decided to call the landline. She wouldn't take him to the café with her, so if she answered, he'd know she was home.

Ilona picked up on the fifth ring with a hesitant, *"Hello?"*

Mark was just about to greet her and start a casual chat when, in the mirror mounted for that very purpose, he saw his boss approaching him.

"So, when are you vacating the premises, ma'am?" Mark asked, pretending he was speaking to a business client. "You remember what we agreed on, right?"

His passing boss gave him a thumbs-up.

Ilona, however, was no longer in a friendly mood.

"You're calling home!" she screamed, recognizing his voice. "Is there something I don't know? Am I supposed to move out? No—you move out! It's because of you I fell into depression!"

Mark wanted to clear up the misunderstanding. Unfortunately, his boss had stopped nearby and was listening in on the conversation. Luckily, he could only hear Mark's side.

"Ma'am, I have everything in writing... There's nothing in the contract in fine print... So please follow through..." Mark hoped Ilona would realize he couldn't speak freely. He was wrong.

"What contract? Our marriage? The only fine print was your dick!"

"So we understand each other perfectly," Mark replied, to the delight of his boss.

He planned to explain the whole situation once he got home. The subject of television was going to be off-limits for the evening—he didn't want to upset Ilona. He still cared about her, despite the weight gain and lost ambition. He still loved her.

At home, he was greeted by a plate of cold, green mush, a switched-off television, and Ilona's gloomy face.

"You should watch more office dramas instead of melodramas—maybe then you'd catch on to how things actually work," he opened, going on the offensive.

"Today is our fifth anniversary," Ilona replied coldly. "I want to mark the occasion—and make sure you remember it. We're starting to eat healthy."

"Oh crap!"

"You'll eat chicken twice a month. Only chicken. Maybe turkey, as a substitute."

"Sweetheart, let's go out to a restaurant. You know how men are—we don't remember dates..."

"You have your friends' birthdays saved in your calendar."

"What calendar? Okay, yes, I have them saved—but on my phone. Have you been snooping through my phone? How do you know the password? You watch too much TV, and then you get these crazy ideas."

Mark ran over to the television and touched it.

"It's hot!" he shouted triumphantly. "You just turned it off!"

"Maybe," Ilona replied. "Or maybe it wasn't me..."

"I know you're upset. I want to make it up to you. Get dressed—we'll go out somewhere... Have a few drinks, laugh a little..."

Ilona stayed silent. The "green mush" had been a revenge plan she'd been brewing for days. She *knew* Mark would forget their anniversary. He didn't even remember his parents' birthdays. He was always so busy.

But when it came to his colleagues, he *did* remember—working hard on maintaining a good image in the company.

What stopped him from saving this one date in his calendar?

Why was work more important?

"On TV..." she began.

"Go ahead and finish—I already know you've been watching it."

"On TV, they were talking today about squeezed lemon syndrome."

"Sweetheart, don't believe the media. I feel great at work. It's something I'm passionate about. I'm like a fish in water, like—"

"Those were the same researchers who talked about how much of our lives we spend watching television."

"So... are we going out? Will you change?" Mark asked, eyeing her stretched-out jeans and oversized T-shirt, clearly meant to hide the folds around her stomach.

"I've got roots showing!"

"No one will notice."

"You always go to places filled with skinny bimbos. *They* will notice."

"Most Polish women are slim. But if you'd rather move than lose weight, we can relocate somewhere where the restaurants are full of hippos."

Ilona didn't respond. He *knew* she had gained weight because she quit smoking. And now he was criticizing her. He was probably having an affair with some skinny girl.

Upset by the thought, she stormed out of the kitchen and locked herself in the bathroom. She sat down on the toilet seat. She felt miserable. Her face was burning, and a lump had formed in her throat. But she didn't cry.

"Are you getting ready?" came a voice from behind the door.

"Yes!" she shouted back.

But she didn't start putting on even the slightest bit of makeup. She didn't feel like going anywhere. Fresh in her memory were the hungry stares of women sizing up her husband.

She took a long shower and changed into her pajamas. She looked in the mirror. Her face looked startled, not indifferent like she had hoped.

"Maybe I should doll myself up and go out alone?" she thought.

The imagined reaction from Mark cheered her up a little.

She walked out of the bathroom.

Mark was sitting on the edge of the couch, already dressed and ready to leave. His eyes widened when he saw her.

"You've never lied to me before!" he said. "And you never played stupid games."

"What are you talking about?" she asked, pretending to be surprised. "It's Monday, six o'clock."

"So you don't care about our anniversary?"

"Our anniversary is on Friday!"

Without saying another word, Mark buttoned up his coat and walked out of the apartment.

Ilona ran after him.

"Where are you going?"

"I'm going to fight the lemon syndrome!" she heard him shout from the stairwell.

Mark took a deep breath of the October air.

It already smelled like burning plastic and other nastiness from the central heating systems.

"The air must be cleaner in the city center," he thought. *(What kind of place do we live in?)*

"At least Ilona's not smoking nearby anymore. That would've made it worse. Oh, right... she quit."

The thing was, they hadn't gone for a walk together in two years, and the version of Ilona that Mark still remembered from their walks was the one who smoked. Back when she still smoked, she would go outside for a cigarette. So, in essence, it was hard to notice the difference—whether she still smoked or not.

But other things *were* noticeable—she had stopped going to work, she had started binge eating, she had become addicted to television, and the only time she left the house was to go shopping.

"What happened to this woman?" Mark wondered.

For the next ten minutes of his walk, he questioned whether it was his fault. Had he said something that crushed her? Or maybe she really did have some kind of actual depression—caused by chemical imbalances in the brain or some kind of deficiency?

Why hadn't he read more about it, or sent her to a proper psychologist?

He had assumed she was just pretending—trying to buy herself time to pursue her dream of writing a screenplay. But he had once checked her laptop and found only five boring pages of a monologue about quitting smoking. He kept checking from time to time, and the page count never increased.

And now these scenes she was starting to cause.

"Okay," he thought, softening a little, "today's scene..."

He couldn't remember Ilona ever throwing tantrums—at least not before she went on medical leave.

In fact, their life now seemed clearly divided into *before* and *after* Ilona went on sick leave.

Before, she was a beautiful, well-groomed woman. Sure, she had that nasty smoking habit—at parties she could go through several packs.

But she was sharp, kind, well-read—really, you could talk to her about almost anything.

She could find common ground with both a lawyer and a kiosk saleswoman (not to insult saleswomen, nor glorify lawyers).

She did tend to speak to people with a certain air of superiority—that was a habit Mark had never liked in her. Now, he actually missed it.

Since she'd stopped working, Ilona had somehow lost her confidence.

She declared she was cutting ties with all her smoker friends so she wouldn't be tempted.

She said she wouldn't go out for a while because people smoked at bus stops, and the temptation would be too strong.

That she wouldn't even go shopping because she might buy a pack and wouldn't be able to admit it to Mark.

"Maybe you could go out with just a little cash—less than the price of a pack?" he suggested, slightly alarmed by the idea of Ilona never leaving the apartment at all.

"Then I'll buy a cigarette off some homeless guy or pick up a butt from the sidewalk," she replied. "You don't know the power of this addiction."

And so it happened that, for the first three months, Ilona left the house only three times—to take out the trash.

Their grocery list began to include junk food: chips, candy, cookies, pastries, cake...

Once, when Mark refused to buy sweets, the list was suddenly filled with flour, sugar, yeast, eggs, margarine, etc.—and two hours after he brought the groceries home, the smell of freshly baked cake filled the apartment.

Almost immediately, the doorbell would ring. Neighbors would show up with some issue they needed to discuss—though Mark knew full well that the real reason for their visits was the smell of cake.

That's why he gave up trying to censor the grocery list. The neighbors' visits were too time-consuming—he couldn't focus on work when they were around.

Besides, they kept encouraging Ilona to "just have one," because they didn't feel like going outside to smoke.

And when they *did* step out, they'd return reeking of burnt nicotine, which visibly irritated Ilona.

At first, Ilona's figure only rounded out slightly.

But after six months, she no longer resembled her former self. And not just in appearance.

She lost interest in sex.

She stopped reading.

And she started watching TV.

It had all started with a commercial for a morning show that promised to cover the topic of quitting smoking.

She woke up at 5:50 a.m. to watch it—and stuck to that routine ever since.

Mark happened to be passing a bus stop when a bus headed toward the city center pulled up.

On impulse, he got on.

He decided, as his role in the situation now demanded, to find a pub and get drunk.

All the places where he might run into colleagues were out of the question.

The rest were mostly filled with teenagers and students.

Eventually, he ended up at a small bar said to be frequented by lawyers.

The drinks were ridiculously expensive, so average drinkers—those who preferred cheaper options—tended to avoid the place.

Mark entered somewhat hesitantly, unsure of what to expect.

The prices had clearly scared off most patrons.

Three booths were occupied by couples. The rest were empty.

At the bar sat two young women in office attire—and, of course, the old man from the gym.

A mild aggressor mode kicked in for Mark. He walked up to the bar, *accidentally* bumping the old man's shoulder.

"Are you hitting on me?" the old man asked. "It's not like it's crowded here."

"Like in ancient times," Mark muttered. "Fewer people back then."

"Ah, it's you. I knew I'd see you again."

"Did you deduce that? Using methods of the ancient Greeks?"

"No. I had a feeling fate put you in my path for a special reason."

"So you weren't afraid of me calling the police—you just had a sense of mission?"

"I'm a family therapist. From your argument with that lovely lady, I gathered that you've got issues. Is she your wife?"

"Do you always butt in when it's not your business?"

"I believe there are certain indicators in this case that support my judgment. Here—my card," the old man said, pulling a piece of cardboard from his wallet and placing it on the bar. He finished the rest of his drink and left without saying goodbye.

Mark noticed that both women and the bartender had been eavesdropping on their conversation.

As soon as the old man left, the bartender came right over and took Mark's order.

"That guy's pretty good," the bartender said into the air. "He's saved a lot of marriages."

"Judging by the price of the drinks, I thought the service here would be more professional," Mark snapped. "And wouldn't stick its nose where it doesn't belong."

"We all know each other pretty well here," said one of the women. "Margaret Smith, psychologist," she added, walking up to Mark and extending her hand. Marek shook it reluctantly. The woman was attractive and gave his body a rather lustful glance.

"And I'm a lawyer, a divorce specialist," said the second woman, also stepping forward to greet him.

"Let me guess—you two work together?"

"Sometimes we refer clients to one another, yes. Some people who come for psychological help end up needing a lawyer. And vice versa—after a divorce, many people need emotional support."

"Don't trust them too much," muttered the bartender, polishing glasses with a cloth.

"I thought I could come here and have a quiet drink," Mark sighed, finishing his cocktail and preparing to leave.

"These are our cards," said Margaret, stuffing something into his hand.

"Take his too," giggled her companion, handing him the old man's card. "Just for a service comparison."

Mark reluctantly took the business cards, stuffed them into his pocket, and walked out. He decided he would tell Ilona the whole story.

She would have laughed at it once—maybe she still would now?

After all, who would have expected *the old man.*

He decided to buy himself a beer from the liquor store and walk home. A few kilometers in the fresh air would definitely do him good.

When he was already near the house, he felt a surge of anger toward his wife. He decided to stop for one more drink at the neighborhood dive bar.

Ilona sat in front of the TV, but the scenes of the movie flickered past her eyes unnoticed.

"Where did he go? With whom?" she kept asking herself. *"What should I say when he comes back? And he didn't even eat dinner... He'll be hungry.. Or maybe he'll go eat with some tramp? I could've made a nice dinner and casually mentioned our Friday anniversary. Why did I make such a scene?"*

One o'clock passed. Ilona turned off the TV and, for the first time in two years, went to bed before him.

Twenty minutes later, she heard Mark coming into the apartment.

He peeked into the bedroom.

"I'll sleep on the sofa," he announced, and shut the door.

In the morning, Ilona overslept.

She woke at 6:30 to the sound of Mark's footsteps as he came in to grab clothes from the wardrobe.

"Go ahead and sleep. You're not going to work, anyway!"

"Oh no!" Ilona jumped out of bed. "There was supposed to be an interview with that writer on the morning show today..."

"But writing is in your blood! Why would you need advice from some writer..."

Ilona got irritated, as she always did when they talked about her (theoretical) writing.

"You think I can't write?"

"I haven't had a chance to read anything yet, so it's hard for me to say."

"But I told you, I ran the student paper back in college."

"As the editor! I remember. But did you actually write anything of your own?"

"You're distracting me!" Ilona brushed past her husband and rushed to the TV.

She plopped down on the still-warm sofa—so he had slept in the apartment after all—and clicked the remote.

The TV didn't respond.

She ran up to the screen and began pressing buttons manually. After a few tries, she managed to find the right one.

She didn't really know how to operate it without the remote.

Commercials were playing.

She padded off to the kitchen to find new batteries.

She slid off the plastic cover of the remote and stared at the empty battery slots for a long moment.

"You jerk!" she shouted, outraged—forgetting that she had promised herself she'd be nice to Mark today.

"You need to break your habits!" came his voice from the bathroom.

Ilona sat down and stared at the screen. The commercials ended, and the interview with the writer began.

Ilona thought the woman was terrible.

But she had published several bestsellers, so Ilona wanted to watch the interview—and hate on her silently.

Oh yes, she was envious.

If not for her depression (which she was slowly starting to believe was real), *she* would have published a bestseller too.

Or written a blockbuster movie script.

"We receive many messages from people asking, 'What's the secret to your success?'" the journalist asked.

"Definitely consistency and narrowing down my interests..."

"Narrowing down interests!" Ilona scoffed.

"Could you explain what you mean by that?" the journalist asked, equally puzzled.

"Maybe I didn't phrase it quite right..."

"And you're a *writer*?" Ilona mocked from the sofa.

"...what I mean is that we should focus on the field we've chosen and not get distracted by other things," the writer explained.

"I used to be overwhelmed with daily work, learning foreign languages—I tried to study five at once—and I also did yoga, pilates, and went to the gym, which took me forty minutes to get to each way..."

"And how did you know that writing was the path to choose, and the field in which you'd succeed?" asked the journalist.

"I didn't know. I just felt it. Sometimes writing brought me joy, sometimes it was torture, but in my mind's eye I saw dozens of my books on bookstore shelves... and I decided to make that happen.

Besides, I was always going on about writing to my friends and even strangers. Until one day, someone asked me how I was doing. I replied, 'I'm writing a book.' And they said, 'You've been saying that for twenty years.'

I did the math—I had met that person twenty years earlier. And clearly, even back then, I was calling my random scribbles 'writing a book.'"

"Sounds familiar!" Mark's voice called from the hallway. "Honey, I'm heading out. No need to cook lunch, I'm afraid of that green mush."

"It was avocado with honey!" Ilona snapped. "Very tasty."

"...that comment was like a catalyst for change," the writer continued.

"I realized I'd become one of those people who talk about doing something instead of actually doing it. I understood that my friends were already bored of my talk about writing and had stopped believing I'd ever succeed."

"How quickly did you write your first book?" the journalist cut in. "I've heard you have a very fast writing pace."

"It's not particularly fast. I write about one page every half hour. Then I take a break. I have to admit I'm still not very organized... I get especially distracted by the internet. That's why I turn it off while I write. Still, I manage about 3.5 to 4 pages a day. That lets me finish a book in three months..."

"And doesn't writing that quickly affect the quality of the text?"

"That's for the readers to judge," the writer replied. "Judging by sales, they seem satisfied."

"What a brazen witch!" Ilona shouted from the safety of her cozy sofa.

"Don't you regret not focusing on language learning instead of writing?"

"I already speak seven. Three at an advanced level, three at intermediate, and I just finished a beginner's course in the seventh."

"Yeah, right!" Ilona yelled. "You probably know them like 'Me eat, me drink'!"

"Which languages?" the journalist asked, somewhat skeptically.

"At an advanced level—English, French, and Norwegian. Intermediate—Russian, German, and Spanish. And beginner—Japanese."

"How long did it take you to learn them?"

"Anywhere from a few years to over a decade. I've been learning English since primary school. But you shouldn't be discouraged by how much time it takes—after all, that time will pass anyway."

"And I bet she has a maid who cooks!" Ilona snorted.

She felt awful. The writer from the show had already published over a dozen books—five of them bestsellers—and two had been adapted into films. And then those seven languages—how did she find the time?

"Maybe she didn't watch TV," Ilona thought. *"But surely she's addicted to the internet."*

"Everyone watches TV!" she began defending her habit. But was she, Ilona, just a typical "everyone"?

She was supposed to be different. She had always considered herself better than her peers—which may have made her a bit arrogant and caused difficulties in forming lasting relationships. But back in high school, no one else read Proust. No one else read philosophy books.

And now those same people were building careers. And not through connections. No. She had to admit that most of them had gotten where they were thanks to their own determination, hard work, and surely many sacrifices—sacrifices she hadn't been able to make.

Whenever she got in touch with them, they would tell her what they were currently up to. Then would come the dreaded question: *"And what about you?"*

To which she always replied that she was writing a screenplay.

Never mind that she had only written five pages in the two years since she'd gone on medical leave. Without fail, she would talk about her script, always adding that she couldn't reveal the plot—because that would kill the creative momentum.

Somehow, her friends never seemed interested in the topic. Apparently, they didn't believe she had it in her.

"Maybe it's because there are no results?" She began analyzing the situation.

"I'll show you what I'm made of!" she declared, jumping off the sofa with determination and marching over to her dusty laptop.

After turning it on, she decided to check her email first.

And just like that, an hour passed—thousands of unread emails had piled up; she hadn't checked her inbox in ages.

Soon, an alarm went off. Surprised—since she hadn't set one—she started looking for the device.

It was hidden in a kitchen drawer, with a little note attached.

She felt a small rush of adrenaline.

Could it be that her *"kitten"* had left her a sweet message?

"Stop writing. 'Maria Izabela in Paris' is starting."

How could she have forgotten about that show! Today was the premiere!

And how did Mark know she'd been waiting for it?

That she'd want to sit down and write at that exact moment?

He really did know her well.

Or was it sarcasm?

The show was starting in ten minutes.

She decided to print out her *"screenplay"* for Mark.

He was sure to love it.

Only five pages, but *so* much happened in them.

A moment later, the freshly printed pages, still smelling of ink, were ready. She loved that scent—just like the smell of books.

But enough sniffing! The show was about to start.

An hour flew by as she watched the Brazilian woman's airport drama.

Then came more episodes, but she watched those from the kitchen.

Mark deserved a proper dinner.

She decided to cook pasta with vegetables and shrimp—his favorite.

They just needed to defrost first... She placed them in hot water.

Normally, she didn't like to defrost food so "extremely," but just this once.

She sautéed the vegetables, cooked the pasta, and ran back to the TV.

A rerun was on—about a screenwriter from New York.

She got so caught up in the episode that she didn't notice Mark had come home.

"Are you divorcing me or the TV?" came a voice from the hallway.

"Dinner will be ready in thirty minutes! We're having shrimp!" Ilona shouted back, continuing to watch, with a touch of envy, the adventures of the screenwriter.

She would have that kind of life too.

Well, maybe not entirely—she already had a wonderful husband.

Shrimp! She suddenly remembered.

After half an hour, the dish was finally ready.

Though she should probably factor in the extra time spent watching TV.

Yes, it had been an hour since Mark got home.

How patient he was, not even asking about dinner.

A real treasure.

She knocked on his study door.

Silence.

"Sweetheart! Dinner's ready! There's shrimp!"

Silence.

Worried, she went to check the bedroom to see if Mark was asleep.

What she saw was apocalyptic—closets torn apart, clothes strewn all over the floor.

Mark was gone.

"What the hell is going on now?" she panicked.

"Maybe he's sick and went to the hospital? And he was just looking for socks? What did he even say when he came in? 'When's dinner?' Or was it something else?"

She grabbed her phone and called Mark. He picked up after the fifth ring.

"Where are you?! Dinner's ready!"

"I moved out."

"Where? To whom?"

"To a lovely lady... Want to talk to her?"

"You pig!" she shouted and hung up.

The phone rang a second later. It was Mark. She didn't answer.

A moment later a text arrived:

"I moved into a hotel. The lovely lady is the receptionist. Do you remember what I asked when I got home from work?"

She didn't. She couldn't remember a thing.

How to get out of this situation? Was he serious or just messing with her?

What was going on? She wondered.

She was supposed to write her script today—or start a new project.

"Well, fuck it all," she muttered to herself.

"To write, you need peace of mind—not drama with lunatics. I wonder when he'll come back?"

Mark didn't return that evening, or the next day.

He didn't send a message or call.

Neither did she—afraid he'd quiz her about what he'd said when he got home.

And so, a week passed.

Mark couldn't forgive her for that.

How could she not hear it?

The word *"divorce"* usually sets off alarm bells.

And she had the nerve to respond with something about shrimp.

At first, it had been meant as a joke, but her indifference sent him into a kind of rage.

He wanted her to suffer—just like he was.

That's why he packed his things quietly—making sure not to make a sound—and tiptoed out of the apartment, gently closing the door behind him.

This wasn't supposed to be the end of their marriage—just a wake-up call.

Let her see what she's losing because of that damn television.

But after her phone call, he started regretting his decision.

Ilona wouldn't beg him to come back.

Her pride wouldn't allow it.

And why on earth did he mention the receptionist?

Now she probably thinks he moved in with some skinny girl.

And that the reason he left was her extra weight, not the months-long TV addiction.

He'd handled it all wrong.

He should've convinced Ilona to go to some kind of rehab program.

Talked to her. Explained how he really felt.

Was it possible such a conversation would have ended in failure?

That the shared language they had developed over years together was gone?

Impossible. Surely, if he just started the conversation right, they'd find a way to connect.

Or maybe not?

Maybe their marriage had actually ended two years ago?

He wanted to call her so many times, but didn't know how to start the conversation without ruining everything for good.

He couldn't attack her—he knew that never worked with Ilona.

But he didn't want to explain himself either.

She should be the one to apologize—for not hearing the word "divorce."

Oh right—she didn't even know he had said it.

And at that moment, Mark would always put down the phone he was holding, ready to call Ilona.

And so, a week passed.

On the seventh day after moving out, Mark found the business cards from the pushy specialists at the bar—and from the old man at the gym.

Maybe the psychologist could help him?

The therapist would've been better, but his eye still hurt from the old man's punch.

Margaret answered the phone immediately.

Her voice was slightly breathless, with a hint of excitement in it.

"I'd be happy to talk with you. Yes, I remember you. I have a free slot this evening, does that work for you?"

Mark agreed, although the late hour made him a little uneasy.

Why so late?

Do psychologists actually work at that time?

Or maybe Ms. Margaret wanted to lure him into a bar—and then into bed?

He couldn't deny she was an attractive woman... but far too forward.

He never liked women like that.

He'd had a few in his life—or rather, *they'd had him*, and then ditched him.

For him, breakups were painful.

They were always rushing toward new thrills, uninterested in the idea of spending a few or even several years with someone like him.

In truth, they had all left him. Every one of his exes.

They had either cheated—or worse, left simply because they were bored with him.

That's why he didn't trust Ilona.

He was suspicious and jealous.

He didn't pick fights over every glance she threw at another man—he bottled up those negative feelings.

At the beginning of their relationship, Ilona had given him plenty of reasons to be jealous.

She flirted with his friends (so he stopped inviting them over), smiled too much at his coworkers (so he stopped taking her to work events), and so on.

For the past two years, things had been calm.

Ilona stayed at home.

But she was still connected to the world—not just through TV, but mostly through the Internet.

Maybe she was sitting at home chatting with some guy from Mozambique?

Maybe she dreamed at night about sex with someone so exotic?

And he, her own husband, had become dull and ordinary—just like he had for all the others?

Or maybe she was writing to some romantic Russian who sent her poems.

They were plagiarized from the internet, of course, but Ilona wouldn't know that—and she'd fall in love.

Or maybe she was chatting with an American?

Dreaming of a Hollywood career he promised her after she sent him the five pages of her script.

Naturally, he never read them, but he liked the way she looked in old photos (the current ones, she probably wouldn't have sent) and tried to seduce her.

But the worst thought was that Ilona was chatting with some *local* guy—and secretly meeting him while Mark was at work.

How else to explain her disinterest in sex?

Maybe she was getting plenty of it in the mornings, while he was off fighting for a promotion and playing office politics.

What was it about him that made women lose interest?

Now his pride could remain intact—*he* was the one who left first. For the first time.

No one had made a fool out of him, no one had turned him into a laughingstock.

And yet, he didn't feel good about it.

He should've handled it differently.

Maybe it wasn't too late?

But how to talk to Ilona now?

How to explain everything to her?

In Margaret's office, he had expected the stereotypical therapist's couch—a chaise lounge where she'd ask him to lie down.

Instead, he sat on a chair beside her desk, across from Margaret herself.

She was wearing a red blazer, a red skirt, a black blouse, and matching black stockings.

Her hair was down (black, just how he liked it), glasses perched on her nose, adding a certain sex appeal, tastefully applied makeup, and perfume.

The same scent Ilona used to wear.

That probably saved him.

If not for that reminder of Ilona, he might've succumbed to this woman's charm.

She would've used him and tossed him aside.

Maybe they had mutual acquaintances who would later giggle at the sight of him and whisper to each other, comparing the length of his penis in centimeters.

"We'll start with a few tests," said Margaret, handing him a stack of papers.

"But these are IQ tests!" Mark protested. "I didn't come here to measure my intelligence—I came for advice! It'll take an hour to finish all this nonsense, you'll charge me, then go home and schedule another appointment for next week. But this is urgent! I could lose my wife!"

"Maybe you should reflect on that relationship if one week apart already means the end of your marriage," Margaret replied sharply, her eyes flashing with irritation.

"Tell me the whole story, but one session is not enough to offer a proper opinion.

Besides, a psychologist never tells a patient what to do. We guide you in a way that helps *you* find your own answers."

"So should I be going to a fortune teller instead?" Mark snapped, frustrated.

He no longer liked Margaret.

She was some kind of hothead, a spitfire—judging by how easily he had rattled her.

And a spiteful one, at that.

Definitely spiteful.

"If you're looking for easy answers... Tell me about your relationship with your wife."

Mark, somewhat reluctantly and stumbling over his words, briefly summarized the incident that led him to move out, along with the motivations behind his decision.

"Now tell me a bit about yourself, so I can have a fuller picture of the situation... Where do you work, what are your life goals, dreams, interests..."

"Is that really important?"

"I get the impression that your wife plays the role of an anchor—one that's keeping you from sailing out of the harbor. I shouldn't be offering such an opinion, but you've clearly asked for it. Maybe it would be better to look at the situation from a different angle? Sometimes it's healthier to leave toxic people behind, even if the separation is painful..."

"You're right—you *shouldn't* be giving your opinion," Mark replied, standing up.

"That'll be 200 złoty, this is a private session... Please give the whole matter some thought. If you'd like to meet again—you have my number."

Marek reached for his phone. He was going to call *her*.

But Ilona's phone was out of range—or turned off.

He called the landline.

A strange woman picked up—it definitely wasn't his wife.

What had happened? Could so much have changed in just one week?

Was someone else now living in their apartment?

"May I speak to Ilona?" He asked.

"She's not here. She went for a walk with her husband."

"But *I'm* her husband—unless there's something I don't know... and I'm definitely *not* on a walk with her..."

"Mr. Marek! There are a lot of things you clearly don't know—like how to treat a woman, for example. This is Marchewska, Ilona's mother."

"Oh fuck!" slipped out of Mark's mouth.

Embarrassed by his own reaction, he hung up.

Just what he needed—*the mother-in-law*.

Five years of marriage and she still called him *Mr.* And of course she had to show up at *this* critical moment. Answering the phone like she lived there full-time.

And lying. Ilona wasn't on a walk with him.

Or maybe she *had* gone out—with someone else.

Someone her mother approved of...

Or maybe Ilona was just sitting in front of the TV at home?

Was she crying or not? He wondered in the silence of his hotel room.

He probably needed to start thinking about renting a flat.

It was a waste to keep burning through his savings on a hotel — and the arrival of his mother-in-law didn't bode well for a quick reconciliation with his wife.

"You haven't called in a month," was all Ilona heard as she opened the door after the relentless pounding.

Her mother stood in the hallway.

"What's going on?" she asked. "I need to know what's going on or I can't sleep at night!"

"Well, I won't be sleeping now either..." Ilona sighed, glancing theatrically at her wrist, which hadn't known a watch in ages.

"It's not like you're rushing off to work."

"Everyone keeps throwing it in my face that I don't work. As if depression were some kind of luxury."

"Depression or not, you could still take care of yourself. Just look at you! When was the last time you dyed your hair? And what is that rag you're wearing?"

"It's pajamas."

"And where's Mr. Marek?"

"He moved out."

"If I saw my husband in gray pajamas every day, I'd run off too. It's clear—it's time for me to step in," her mother declared, dramatically picking up empty wine bottles from the floor and nudging pizza boxes with her foot.

"Mom, you don't have to meddle in everything."

"Someone has to shake you up. Look in the mirror—ten centimeters of roots, twenty-five extra kilos, and some gray flannel instead of lace."

"Lace is out of fashion now," Ilona managed to interject.

"...and your legs aren't even shaved!" her mother shouted. "And you're surprised he left? And why is it so quiet in here? Did someone die? Why is the TV off? Is it broken?"

Since Mark had left, the TV had remained off.

Ilona sat on the sofa, blankly staring at the black screen, munching on peanuts, pizza, and washing it down with wine.

Once her mother turned the TV on, the living room filled with life again.

Who needs Mark? There are so many great guys out there.

Like that one in the commercial.

But why is *he* with such a stick-thin woman? That girl doesn't even have thighs.

Her nose sticks out of her skinny face.

Ilona dragged herself off the sofa and walked over to the mirror.

She pulled open her robe.

Nope. This didn't look good either.

Her thighs were four or six times the size of the woman's in the commercial.

Rolls on her back and stomach.

Cellulite.

"This so-called depression of yours is just an excuse," said her mother suddenly, entering the room. "You just don't know what to do with your life. My God, child, just look at yourself!"

Ilona quickly wrapped the robe tightly around her.

"I'm decades older than you, but I've never let myself go like this."

"I quit smoking!" Ilona shouted. "Did anyone even notice that?"

"If you measure it by weight gain, then yes, it's very noticeable."

"Mom, you're terrible at comforting people. Go home. I'll go crazy if you stay here."

"You don't need comforting. You need a wake-up call. Why are you always glued to the TV? Get dressed, go for a walk."

"People stare at me when I walk because I'm too fat."

"Then put on a workout DVD. Don't have one? So you haven't even thought about losing that weight? It's not going to come off on its own."

Ilona didn't reply.

Instead, she began changing TV channels with theatrical indifference.

Her mother sighed in frustration.

A few days passed.

During that time, Ilona spent entire days in front of the television.

Her mother cooked, went grocery shopping, and cleaned.

Ilona gave up her bed, sleeping on the sofa instead.

At the end of the week, Ilona's mother came in one evening with a bottle of vodka.

"Mom, but you don't drink!"

"Drink—and talk like you're at confession. What really happened?"

"I can't."

They drank half the bottle together, making cocktails.

Ilona remained diplomatically silent, and in the end, broke down in tears and went to sleep on the sofa.

In the morning, she heard some shuffling in the living room.

She was still a little drunk and didn't feel like checking where the sounds were coming from.

She lay with her eyes closed, trying to remember where she was.

Then she fell asleep again.

She woke up with a sudden gasp for air.

The apartment was suspiciously quiet.

And the living room... strangely empty.

"Where's the TV?!" Ilona screamed.

The TV stand was bare.

Cables and the remote lay on the floor.

The empty wall loomed before her, promising long, lonely days.

Ilona rushed to the bedroom. Empty.

She opened the closet. Her mother's things were gone.

She felt a wave of anxiety wash over her—the same kind she used to get when she was addicted to cigarettes and, for some reason, couldn't have one.

Not only had the TV disappeared, but the hangover from the night with her mother had also kicked in. She walked over to the fridge, but found nothing that could soothe the emptiness inside her, or the strange fear that had settled around her.

She sat down on the sofa, analyzing her emotions.

She hadn't watched anything on TV for the past few weeks, but she could always press the button on the remote and dive into the world of her favorite characters. She had a choice.

Now that choice had been taken from her.

But she wasn't going to let that slide. She grabbed her phone and dialed the police.

The officer on the other end listened, somewhat surprised, to her story about the disappearing television set.

"Would you like to report a break-in?"

"I suspect I know who the culprit is."

"I'm listening."

"It's my mother."

"You want to report your mother? How much was the TV worth?"

"Probably not much, it was an old model. But I'm reporting it on principle."

"Principles and criminal law are two different things. What exactly happened?"

"I don't remember. My mother got me drunk and I don't remember what might've happened."

"Maybe you sold the TV yourself. Try to remember. I'm not filing a report."

That would have irritated even the most devoted Stoic, and Ilona had never practiced that philosophical doctrine. She dialed her mother's number.

Her mother picked up after five rings.

"I hope you're feeling better?" she said.

"I felt much better before your invasion. Give back the TV!"

Silence fell on the other end.

"If you don't return it, I'll call the police again. They're just waiting for my confirmation to issue a warrant for your arrest."

"Do you need a photo? The police ones are usually pretty lousy."

"I'll give them the one where you weighed 30 kilos more!" Ilona shouted.

A knock on the door enraged her even more. She rushed over and flung it open.

Standing in the hallway was the old man from the gym — the same one who had given Marek a black eye. Ilona, stunned, slammed the door shut.

"What's going on over there?" her mother asked on the other end of the line.

The knocking sounded again.

"I've got a strange situation here. I'll call you back in a few minutes. And don't think this matter is over!"

Her mother's chuckle before hanging up threw her off balance.

She opened the door again.

She probably wasn't having any post-alcohol hallucinations — and if she was, they were pretty convincing.

"If you want some kind of compensation, please take it up with my husband and stop harassing me."

"Your husband already paid me. That's why I'm here."

Ilona looked suspiciously at the old man. Maybe he had memory problems? But how did he get her address?

The old man stood there smiling. He looked very sure of himself.

Only after a moment did the smile fade.

"Your husband didn't tell you anything? That wasn't our agreement."

He pulled a business card from his pocket and handed it to Ilona.

"Please call. I sent you a letter a few days ago. It contains a few more details about the matter."

The man turned and briskly ran down the stairs.

Ilona slammed the door shut. What kind of lunatics was she surrounded by?

In the fridge lay a half-liter bottle of mineral water.

"That's a bit too little for a hangover," Ilona quickly diagnosed.

She decided to change out of her pajamas into jeans and a T-shirt and head to the nearby corner shop for a few bottles of drinks.

The T-shirt fit, but the jeans became a drama.

No, they hadn't shrunk.

She had gained a few more kilos again.

She tried to order food delivery, but for some unknown reason, the estimated waiting time was several hours.

She looked in the mirror.

The pajamas basically looked like sweatpants.

Besides, what could possibly happen in the hundred meters to the shop?

At this hour, most people were at work, kids were at school or hiding out somewhere skipping class.

And the local gossipers probably wouldn't be surprised by anything.

She pulled a baseball cap over her eyes, shoved her debit card into her pajama pants — because her elegant going-out bag didn't match her current haute couture — and stepped outside.

In front of the building, two tipsy men were hauling away her television.

That sight gave her a sudden surge of energy.

"That's my TV!" she shouted and lunged to retrieve her property.

"Calm down, lady — we were here first!" one of the guys protested.

"You don't understand! My mother put it out so my husband would come back to me!"

The men looked at each other.

"She's really spinning some tale," one of them remarked.

"Maybe you need some medical help?" the other asked seriously.

"You'll be the ones needing help if you don't give it back!"

"And since when are we on a first-name basis? You know threats can be punishable by law," snapped the first man.

"Hi, Ilonka!"

Ilona turned around. Behind her stood long-legged Agnes, her former high school friend — the object of every guy's desire, except for Mark. Or at least, that's how it used to be.

"I thought you were still with Mark. Or is it one of these gentlemen?" she giggled maliciously.

The scene probably looked a bit deranged. Definitely not something any South American screenwriter would come up with — and yet life had played her this kind of trick. Ilona considered some kind of poetic comeback, but it turned out the new "owners" of the TV had a human side after all.

"If you really want to know, my name's Mietek," said one of them.

"And I'm Stefan," added the other.

"Details like that don't interest me," Agnes's nose lifted toward the sky. That must be where the expression "sticking your nose in the air" came from, Ilona thought.

But that wasn't the end of her misfortunes.

Agnes pulled out some new model of phone and began filming Ilona in front of the two men, who had frozen in a picturesque pose with the TV.

"Hey loves, you won't believe who I ran into today. Yes, it's *that* Ilonka, the one who wanted to be a screenwriter. Caught her arguing with some bums. Quite the downfall, don't you think?"

"I didn't give consent to have my image published," said Stefan.

"Me neither," added Mietek.

"I'll give you a bottle of cheap wine, even two. But I *have* to post this online," Agnes looked determined.

The men set the TV down.

"Give us that phone," Mietek said sternly. Agnes shrugged and sashayed off toward the shop.

"If she posts it, I'm going to jail!" Mietek shouted.

The men clearly cared about remaining anonymous — though Agnes wasn't moved by that.

Stefan ran after her and snatched her handbag.

Meanwhile, Ilona struggled to lift her plasma TV and made her way toward the front entrance.

"Thief! They're stealing!" Agnes screamed.

"Thief! Robber!" Mietek shouted as he saw Ilona walking off with the TV.

"You're the robber!" Agnes yelled back.

The window of the neighborhood's biggest gossip cracked open. An elderly woman looked down at them.

"I've lived here for decades, and I've never once called the police. But now I've lost track of who's stealing from whom. They'll be here in two minutes — I think they even placed a bet with two patrol cars to see who gets here first."

Ilona had made it to the front door. That's when she realized... she forgot her keys.

With resignation, she handed the TV back to Mietek.

Stefan, meanwhile, was rummaging through Agnes's handbag, but the phone wasn't there. Frustrated, he dumped the entire contents into the neighborhood "fountain" and walked off after Mietek.

The police indeed arrived within two minutes.

The officers gave Ilona and her pajama pants a suspicious once-over.

"She'll confirm those two guys stole my wallet," Agnes announced, pulling the phone — which she had kept in her pocket all along — and started filming the new scene.

"No one stole anything from her," Ilona said.

"She's their accomplice!" Agnes snapped.

Ilona decided to remain diplomatically silent. She reached into her pajama pocket and realized she didn't have her keys or phone. The only thing she had on her was an unsigned debit card.

This did not endear her to the police officers.

"Have you ever ridden in a police car before?" one of the officers asked.

"Not yet."

"Well, you can add it to your list of life achievements once this is all cleared up. Anyone can rent a limo."

"She definitely can't!" Agnes chimed in.

"We're going to have to ask you to delete the recording," the officer said to her.

"I have the right to film."

"Then you're also invited into the police car."

"For what?"

"For being a witness."

"I'll add that to my list too!" Agnes replied.

There was silence in the police car for a while. Agnes was the first to speak.

"Listen, maybe you need help? This all looks pretty bad."

"I live in this housing estate."

"Where? In the stairwell? I can't even afford rent here."

Ilona chose not to answer.

But Agnes kept talking.

"If you want, I can organize a fundraiser for you. And what happened to your fiancé?"

"He became my husband."

The more Ilona tried to explain the situation, the more unbelievable it sounded. So she stopped answering Agnes's questions.

Agnes looked a little sad.

When the police car pulled up in front of the station, she told the officers she was withdrawing her complaint. She also slipped Ilona a small piece of paper with her phone number on it.

Mark answered the phone from the police officer on the sixth ring. He sounded out of breath.

Ilona froze in her chair. What is he doing? This wasn't his usual time for the gym. He's probably having fun with someone.

"Ilona was arguing on the sidewalk about a television? Yes, that sounds like her."

"Does your wife suffer from any mental health issues?"

"No, she doesn't have any disorders. Just an obsession with 42 inches."

"Excuse me?" The officer was clearly confused, seemingly trying to picture a 42-inch length.

"Maybe 14?" he asked, puzzled.

"It was a big TV."

Half an hour later, I walked into the police station waiting room.

Trailing behind me was the old man who had been giving me boxing lessons for the past few weeks.

Ilona sat with her head down, looking like the guiltiest person in the entire corridor.

"Hi, wife. I'm glad to see you."

"Sorry for the trouble," Ilona replied.

"We heard about the trouble. All 42 inches of it," the desk officer called out from his little booth.

Ilona blushed.

We quickly stepped outside.

"I don't have my keys," she said.

"I've got mine."

The walk home passed in silence—even the old man said nothing.

In front of our building, two shady-looking guys were standing with our television.

When they saw Ilona, they started clapping.

"They let you out, bravo."

"Do you know them?" I asked, suspicious.

"They took my TV."

"We can sell it," one of them offered.

"No need," Ilona replied. "I have everything I need. I think."

She looked at me with her blue eyes, tinged with navy.

"We're taking this junk," said the second guy. "Without the TV, you'll qualify for child benefits faster."

Laughing, the bastards walked off with our 42-inch screen.

And finally, it was just the two of us.

Almost.

"You two need to learn how to communicate!" the old man shouted just as we were about to kiss.

"Child benefits can wait," I sighed. "For now, I guess we're adopting you."

Then I doubled over after he elbowed me in the ribs.

Also by K. E. Adamus

Losers: Short Stories
Nieudacznicy. Opowiadania
To Outwit the Fate
The Monk
Sanity Test
Granice Rozumu
Last Episode